Rebecca's Journey Home

by Brynn Olenberg Sugarman

illustrated by Michelle Shapiro

This **PJ BOOK** belongs to

PJ Library®

JEWISH BEDTIME STORIES and SONGS

KAR-BEN
PUBLISHING

KAR-BEN PUBLISHING, INC.
A division of Lerner Publishing Group
241 First Avenue North
Minneapolis, MN 55401 U.S.A.
1-800-4KARBEN

Website address: www.kar-ben.com

Library of Congress Cataloging-in-Publication Data

Sugarman, Brynn Olenberg, 1961–
    Rebecca's journey home / by Brynn Olenberg Sugarman ; illustrations by
Michelle Shapiro.
        p.   cm.
    Summary: Mr. and Mrs. Stein and their young sons Gabe and Jacob adopt a
baby girl from Vietnam.
    ISBN-13: 978–1–58013–157–5 (lib. bdg. : alk. paper)
    ISBN-10: 1–58013–157–3 (lib. bdg. : alk. paper)
    [1. Adoption—Fiction. 2. Vietnamese Americans—Fiction. 3. Jews—United
States—Fiction.] I. Shapiro, Michelle, 1961– ill. II. Title.
PZ7.S94385Reb 2006
[E]—dc22   2005020909

PJ Library Edition ISBN 978-0-7613-4219-9

Manufactured in Hong Kong
4-44781-10213-10/2/2017

041827.5K5/B1192/A6

For Rachele, whose story I have told, and for
her brothers, Aviv and Idan, my husband Dov,
and our entire family, who have been so supportive
of our adoption journey—B.O.S.

To my son, Nathan—M.S.

"Is today the day?"
Jacob asked his
mother excitedly.

"Yes! Today is the day I leave for Vietnam. Soon you will meet your baby sister!" she replied.

It was exactly a year since the Stein family had started their adoption. Mrs. Stein had always wanted to adopt a baby. She loved her two boys, Jacob and Gabriel, very, very much. It had felt warm and wonderful each time she had a baby in her belly. But she also knew there was another way to build a family. That was to share their home with a child who was already born. There were so many babies and children in the world whose parents had loved them but could not take care of them. Mrs. Stein wanted to be the mother of one of those children.

Mr. Stein agreed. He would be happy to have a little girl calling him Daddy. So after many months of telephone calls, meetings, and signing papers, the moment had arrived.

All the documents were ready. It was time for Mrs. Stein to hug her family and board an airplane. She was going far away, to a country called Vietnam, where a baby was waiting to become a member of the Stein family. Her name was Le Thi Hong, but they would give her another name, the English name Rebecca Rose.

Every Friday night during the previous year, when the sun had set, the Steins would stand around the Shabbat table. It was set with candlesticks, grape juice, and two loaves of challah. Delicious smells from the kitchen would be in the air. The family would sing "Shalom Aleichem," welcoming Shabbat, and Mr. and Mrs. Stein would bless their children.

"Don't forget Baby Rebecca!" Jacob had reminded them last week. And so Mr. and Mrs. Stein had faced toward Vietnam, held their hands atop an imaginary little head, and said the traditional blessing for little girls: "May God make you kind and righteous like the first mothers of our people, Sarah, Rebecca, Rachel, and Leah." Even though Baby Rebecca wasn't Jewish yet, receiving her parents' blessing was a good first step.

"Soon Baby Rebecca won't be Vietnamese anymore. She'll be Jewish," Gabe had said. He was four years old and wanted to be an astronaut when he grew up. He had told his preschool class all about Baby Rebecca.

"No! She'll be Vietnamese *and* Jewish," said Jacob who was almost eight. "You can be two things."

"Jacob is right," said his mother. "You can be many things. Baby Rebecca will always be Vietnamese. Her hair will always be straight and black, her skin golden brown, and her eyes the shape of almonds. We'll read her stories about Vietnam to teach her that it is a special place. One day, we will all visit her homeland.

"But she will also be part of the Jewish people and will learn our history, celebrate our holidays, and visit Israel.

"And of course, she will be American!"

For a long time, the Steins had only one picture of their baby. It had been taken when she was born, and she looked very fuzzy, like all newborn babies. But now she was five months old. What did she look like now? the boys wondered. Then, just a week before Mrs. Stein was getting ready to leave, an envelope arrived from Vietnam with a new photograph. Everyone oohed and aahed, and copies of the picture were made for family and friends. But Jacob and Gabriel kept the original, and they would look at it every day.

Mrs. Stein's suitcase had been packed for nearly a month. She'd known that she could get a phone call from Vietnam at any time. The suitcase was full of tiny T-shirts and pink dresses for Rebecca. There was a whole stack of important papers called documents. There were boxes of toys that members of the synagogue had donated for the children at the orphanage.

And Mrs. Stein had packed tiny candlesticks
and candles, so that she and Rebecca could
celebrate their first Shabbat together.

Mrs. Stein had a long journey ahead of her. It took 17 hours to fly from Oregon to California to Japan to Thailand to Vietnam. When she finally stepped off the plane, she was in another world, where the streets were crowded with bicycles, colorful outdoor markets, and golden statues of Buddha.

Every day, the boys looked forward to their mother's e-mails. While she was waiting for the baby, Mrs. Stein was touring the country and shopping for interesting gifts – wooden instruments shaped like frogs, silk robes, and a dragon water puppet. But Jacob and Gabriel knew the best gift of all would be the new baby.

Finally, Baby Rebecca was brought to the hotel. Mrs. Stein took many pictures and express mailed them to the family. There was Baby Rebecca — smiling in a bouncy baby seat,

sitting in her new
mother's lap riding
in a rickshaw,

and wrapped in
a towel after
her bath.

At last, the day arrived for Mrs. Stein and Baby Rebecca to come home. The family arrived at the airport early and waited eagerly until they saw Mrs. Stein, walking like a queen down the carpeted hallway. Little Rebecca was in a pouch, pressed to her tummy like a baby kangaroo. Jacob and Gabriel hopped up and down while everybody hugged.

"I want to hold her!" Gabriel shouted.

"Me first, I'm older!" Jacob argued.

"Hey, what about me?" Mr. Stein asked.

"When we get home, everyone will have a turn," Mrs. Stein said. "You can even get a turn changing her diapers," she added with a wink.

"No thanks!" Jacob replied. "That can be Gabe's job."

Two days later, at Shabbat dinner, the Steins finally got to lay their hands on a real little girl's head as they said the Shabbat blessing for their new daughter.

Soon Baby Rebecca was sitting up all by herself. She knew how to say "goo" and "gah." She liked to smash her rattle against her own head. Jacob and Gabe found this amusing but not very smart. When she slept, she sucked on her pointer and middle fingers together, while her other hand covered her eyes. When she laughed, her black eyes sparkled.

Mr. and Mrs. Stein were busy filling out papers to make Baby Rebecca an American citizen, and they were meeting with the rabbi to arrange her conversion to Judaism.

Just before her first birthday, the family brought Rebecca to the mikvah, the ritual bath. Inside was a small, warm pool. Mr. Stein carried the baby down the steps and gently placed her in the water while the rabbi recited blessings. She was given the Hebrew name Rivka Shoshanah. Mr. and Mrs. Stein promised to give their daughter a Jewish education and raise her to love Shabbat and the holidays.

Now the baby had three names. She had a Vietnamese name: Le Thi Hong. She had an English name: Rebecca Rose. And she had a Hebrew name: Rivka Shoshanah.

She was Vietnamese, American, and Jewish.

"And she'll be many more things someday," Mrs. Stein said.

"Maybe a mother like you," Jacob suggested.

"Or an astronaut like me," Gabe added.

"Or a famous poet, Olympic skier, and mathematician all rolled into one!" Mr. Stein said with a smile.

"You can't be all of those things!" Jacob protested.

"You can be as many things as you want to be. Or at least you can try," his dad replied.

And with a smile and a shake of her rattle,
Baby Rebecca agreed.